ORCHARD BOOKS
338 Euston Road, London NW1 3BH
Orchard Books Australia
Level 17/207 Kent Street, Sydney, NSW 2000

First published in 2009 by Orchard Books

ISBN 978 1 40830 233 0 (HB)
ISBN 978 1 84616 610 5 (PB)

Text © Chris d'Lacey 2009
Illustrations © Adam Stower 2009
The rights of Chris d'Lacey to be identified as the author
and Adam Stower to be identified as the illustrator of this
work have been asserted by them in accordance with the
Copyright, Designs and Patents Act, 1988.

A CIP catalogue record for this book
is available from the British Library.
1 3 5 7 9 10 8 6 4 2
Printed in Great Britain
Orchard Books is a division of Hachette Children's Books,
an Hachette UK company.
www.hachette.co.uk

The Dragon

Waywa

Cresce

Chris d'Lacey

The Dragons of Wayward Crescent

GAUGE

ORCHARD BOOKS

For Chloe and Freya

Chapter One

Burning. Lucy Pennykettle could definitely smell burning. This was not unusual in her house at Number 42 Wayward Crescent, Scrubbley. Lucy's mother, Liz, made clay dragons for a living, and as anybody knows, dragons breathe fire – well, some of Liz's special dragons did, anyway. The fires these dragons breathed were usually quite harmless. They took the form of smoke rings or breathy little *hrrrs*. But this form of burning, the one that was making Lucy's nostrils twitch, seemed to be coming directly from the kitchen. It smelled very much like toast to her.

"Mum!" she shouted and came charging down the stairs in her pyjamas and hedgehog-shaped slippers.

Lucy's mum was on the phone in the front room of the house. She was chattering away 'nineteen to the dozen' as people sometimes say, and clearly hadn't heard Lucy or even smelt the burning. Still calling out to her, Lucy hurried on past and into the kitchen. Sure enough, there were two slices of bread toasting under the grill of the cooker. They were curling at the edges and turning black. Lucy balled her fists. Bravely, she ran to the cooker and turned off the gas. But as the jets of blue flame disappeared to nothing, there was a gentle *whumph* and the toast itself set alight.

Lucy gasped and jumped back. "Mum!" she cried again. "There's a fire in the kitchen!" She glanced at the tall green dragon that always sat on top of the fridge. He was a listening dragon, with ears like rose petals. He put on a pair of small round spectacles and craned his neck towards the cooker.

"Do something!" said Lucy.

The listener sent out an urgent *hrrr*. Within seconds another dragon had zipped into the kitchen to land with a skid and a bump on the worktop. His name was Gruffen. He was a guard dragon.

Lucy sighed with relief. "Gruffen, put the fire out."

Gruffen studied the flames. The scaly ridges above his eyes came together in a frown. Strange as it might seem, Gruffen had never actually seen a fire before. He was a young dragon, still learning how to puff smoke rings from the back of his throat. He could see there was a problem, but wasn't really sure what the solution might be. The toast made a cracking noise. A tongue of flame crept over the grill pan.

Lucy gave a little squeal. "Do something!" she repeated.

Gruffen leapt into action: he tapped his claws and consulted his book.

When Liz made one of her special dragons, it was not unusual for them to come with some kind of 'magical' object. In Gruffen's case this was a book. A sort of manual of dragon procedures. A directory of things to do in awkward situations.

He quickly looked up *'fire'*. There were lots of interesting entries. *Dragon's spark*, said one, *the spirit or life-force of the dragon, born from the eternal fire at the centre of the Earth.* That made his eye ridges lift. *Source of warming*, said another. *Used in cooking*, said a third. And then there was a rather large entry in red: *WARNING – fire can be dangerous to humans, but dragons may swallow it without fear (or hiccoughs).* There was his answer. Gruffen slammed his book shut and flew to the grill.

With one enormous in-breath he sucked the fire towards him and swallowed it completely. The fire was immediately put out and the kitchen was saved. The only

problem was Gruffen breathed in so
hard that the toast came flying off
the grill, smashed against his nose
and exploded in a fine shower of
brittle black crumbs. Liz arrived in
the kitchen seconds later to find that
her normally rosy-cheeked,
straw-haired daughter was
now the colour
of charcoal.

"Oh dear," said Liz, wafting a hand beneath her nose. "Perhaps we'd better have cereal for breakfast instead today."

"That's not funny," Lucy said sourly. "I called you twice."

"Henry Bacon rang," Liz explained, taking a damp cloth to Lucy's face. "I didn't expect him to be on the phone so long, but you know what he's like."

Lucy grunted like a farmyard pig. Henry Bacon, the Pennykettles' grumpy next-door neighbour, was always causing problems. "What did he want?"

"He called to say that the Town Council are planning to demolish the library clock."

"What for?"

"Because it's old and doesn't work very well."

"It tells the wrong time," Lucy agreed. "And it clunks instead of chiming."

"Then it should be fixed, not demolished," Liz said airily. "That clock is part of Scrubbley's history. People would miss it. It's not right to take it down."

Lucy gave a little shrug. "What about the ghost?"

Her mother laughed. "Ghost? What ghost?"

On the worktop, Gruffen looked up 'ghost'. *Strange spectral creatures,* his book informed him. *Often found at a place of great unhappiness*.

"Miss Baxter says it's haunted," Lucy sniffed. Miss Baxter, Lucy's teacher, knew about such things. She often went on visits to stately homes. She claimed she had once seen the ghost of Henry the Eighth eating a chicken drumstick in a cloakroom. Miss Baxter, it had to be said, was slightly strange.

Liz walked away, shaking her bright red hair. "The only thing that haunts that clock tower is pigeons."

"Dead pigeons?" said Lucy, aghast, her mind dizzy with images of phantasmal birds going "coo" (or would it be "woo" if they were ghosts?) as they flew through walls.

"Just pigeons," said her mum a little more soberly. She looked out of the window and became thoughtful for a second. "It would be such a shame to see that clock go. I feel as if I ought to be doing more to save it…"

Lucy glanced at the dragons and they at her. For they all knew what was in Liz's mind. Whenever Lucy's mum became concerned about something, she only ever followed one course of action. She made a new dragon.

A special one.

Chapter Two

Sure enough, Liz started one later that night when Lucy had gone to bed.

Along the landing next door to Lucy's bedroom was a small rectangular room which Liz called her pottery 'studio', though its popular name was the Dragons' Den.

At the window end was a sturdy wooden bench, where Liz kept her paintbrushes and potters' turntable and all the things she needed for making dragons. The two longer walls were taken up with shelving racks, upon which stood a large number of completed dragons. Most of these were in storage, waiting to be sold on the market in Scrubbley, though some were treasured ornaments and some...well, some, like Gruffen, could spread their wings and move around if they wanted to.

In appearance, most of the Pennykettle dragons looked the same. Their glaze was a mid to bottle-green colour, with occasional streaks of blue or turquoise. And they all had spiky wings and curving tails and oval-shaped eyes and trumpet-like noses. Liz enjoyed sculpting them in different poses. She had dancing dragons, sporting dragons, baby dragons breaking out of their eggs – dragons in all sorts of appealing stances. But those dragons that were special appeared without conscious effort, as though they had simply popped out of Liz's dreams. This is how it was with the dragon that came to be known as Gauge.

Lucy Pennykettle, like her mum, had an unerring instinct for the birth of a special dragon. As Liz was twisting the turntable back and forth, carefully admiring her latest creation, Lucy slipped into the Den.

"You're supposed to be in bed," her mother said.

Lucy tactfully ignored her and came to stand by the bench. She peered at the dragon. "It's a 'he'," she said, gently stroking his 'top knot' – the little spike that rose like a fin from the top of a dragon's head. "What does he do?"

"I don't know," Liz replied. "But he's definitely special. I was just daydreaming and there he was."

"Why's he got a paw missing?" Lucy pointed to the dragon's left arm. The paw at the end of it seemed to be only half there. But as the moonlight shifted across

the window she saw that he was
wearing a kind of waistcoat and
dipping his paw into a shallow
pocket. "He's got something," she
said. Her eyes glowed
with excitement.

Her mother hummed in acknowledgement. "Well, if you want to know what it is, you'd better hurry off downstairs, hadn't you?"

Lucy was gone in a flash. She knew exactly what her mother meant. In the freezer compartment of the fridge was a small plastic box with a pale blue lid. Inside the box was, of all things, a snowball. Liz had kept it since she was a girl. There were many secrets surrounding this nugget of ice, and even Lucy didn't know all of them. But the snow was what brought her mother's dragons to life. That was all that mattered to Lucy.

She scooted upstairs and handed the box over. Liz opened the lid, letting a fine wisp of condensation escape. The snowball glistened in the moonlight. Lucy held her breath as her mother broke off the tiniest chunk and let it rest on the new dragon's snout. Immediately, it melted inside his nostrils.

"There, the kilning process is started," said Liz. Then she turned the dragon until he was facing a tall, elegant female dragon who sat alone on a shelf just behind the bench. Her name was Guinevere. Liz whispered something to her in the ancient language of dragontongue. Guinevere's eyes slid open.

Lucy's shoulders bristled with excitement. She had always wanted to know what happened next, but the most she ever saw was a violet light shining out of Guinevere's eyes. That was all she saw this time as well. The light played over the new dragon's body, creating what looked like a slight halo of fire around him.

Her mother turned Lucy away then, saying, "Come on. Guinevere will hurr when he's ready. Oh, by the way, while you were downstairs a name came to me."

"Really?" said Lucy. This was quite unusual. Dragons weren't usually named until they were active.

"I think he's got a watch in his pocket," said Liz, "because the name I thought of was Gauge."

Lucy didn't look impressed. "Gauge?" she queried.

"It's a word that means 'to measure'."

"What's he going to measure – with a watch?"

"Time, I suppose."

Lucy's shoulders sank. "That's boring," she tutted.

But, as was usual where special dragons were concerned, she was in for a few surprises.

Chapter Three

It was another two days before
Guinevere signalled to the listening
dragon and he, in turn, signalled to
Liz to say that Gauge was ready. Liz
was in the kitchen at the time,
having a cup of tea with Mr Bacon.
Henry did not believe in dragons,

so he did not hear the listener's hurr. But he was close enough to feel a warm draught in his left ear, which prompted him to enquire if Mrs P, as he called Liz, had left a gas ring on?

She said she had not and it was just a dragon breathing. That made Henry frown and caused Lucy to stifle a laugh. They enjoyed teasing Henry, though care was needed when a new dragon was in the house. Young special dragons had to be taught that they needed to act like solid clay figures when humans were near.

While Lucy dashed upstairs to see what was happening, Liz carried on chatting to Henry. "Go on. You were talking about the plans to get rid of the library clock. Why can't the Council just mend it?"

"Far too costly," Mr Bacon said, winkling a finger round his hairy ear canal.

"It's surely cheaper than knocking it down and installing a new one?"

Henry shook his head. "Needs specialist attention. Old workings. Cranky. Cheaper to rip it out and put in a digital display."

Liz sighed in dismay. "We can't have flashing neon bulbs in the middle of an old market town like Scrubbley. It's completely out of character. I shall protest. And so will others."

But to her further dismay, Henry leaned forward and said, "Too late, Mrs P. Word has it that the motion has already been passed. Rubber-stamped behind closed doors." He beat his fist down lightly on the table, enough to make his tea cup rattle against its saucer.

Liz folded her arms (never a good sign) and let out a little puff of disgust. "Well, the ghost won't like it!"

"Ghost?" said Henry, closing one eye.

Liz tapped her foot. Goodness, she thought, she had turned into Lucy in the space of a few seconds. "The clock tower's…haunted," she said.

"Poppycock!" cried Henry, slapping his thigh. "Worked in that library twenty years, Mrs P. Never seen a spectre or heard the slightest hint of wailing – apart from the time Miss Hickinbottom dropped a large encyclopaedia on her toe."

"Well, if I were the Town Council, I'd be careful," said Liz. "You shouldn't mess about with the supernatural."

Henry drummed his fingers. "No such thing as the supernatural," he declared, just as a dragon fluttered into the kitchen and landed on the three long hairs of his nearly bald head. "What the...?" he cried. He jumped in his chair and felt his bald spot. But by then, Gauge had

29

fluttered onto the fridge top to say
hello to the listener.

"Mum, I couldn't control him!"
Lucy cried, appearing, out of breath,
at the kitchen door.

"What hit me?" said Henry,
starting to look around.

Liz sighed heavily and snapped her fingers to get Henry's attention. As their eyes met, Liz's gaze became a strange hypnotic stare and the colour of her eyes turned from green to violet. "Go home, Henry. Have a nice sleep," she said.

A dizzy look spread across Henry's face. He rose up like a robot and was gone.

"Sorry," Lucy said sheepishly to her mum.

"It's all right," Liz said, letting her eyes return to green. "Henry won't remember a thing." She glanced at the meeting taking place on the fridge top. She spoke in dragontongue to Gauge, who fluttered down to her open hand.

"You need to learn the house rules – and quickly."

Gauge flicked his tail and looked at her with wide, admiring eyes. He dipped his hand into his waistcoat pocket and, just as Liz had predicted, brought out a watch. He gave a gentle questioning *hrrr*.

"You want to know how quickly?" Liz translated.

Gauge gave a nod.

Liz glanced through the window. "By the time it gets dark?" she suggested, wondering if he would even understand the concept of sunrises and sunsets at his tender age. Though you could never tell with dragons. Sometimes, they could do or know extraordinary things. And so it was with Gauge.

He flipped open his watch and stared at its display. Liz and Lucy leaned forward to share a look.

"That's not a watch," said Lucy. For there were no hands or numbers or date window to see. Instead, they had glimpsed what appeared to be a miniature solar system of planets whirling around one another. And possibly some stars. All deeply reflected in Gauge's eyes.

Liz nodded in astonishment. "I think that's more than a watch," she said. "I think it's a kind of tuning device."

"Pardon?" said Lucy. She was now completely confused.

"I think this dragon is in touch

with the universe," Liz said.

And to answer Liz's question, Gauge said that nightfall was predicted in eight earthly hours, twelve earthly minutes and ten earthly seconds – though he wasn't quite sure, yet, what that meant. He flipped the watch shut.

"He's weird," said Lucy. "What use is a dragon that times things?"

"I don't know," said Liz, but her thoughts, like the planets in Gauge's watch, were steadily whirring. And though she couldn't see how Gauge could possibly help with it yet, those thoughts kept returning to the problem of saving the library clock.

Chapter Four

In the meantime, however, Lucy's question, "What use is a dragon that times things?" was quickly answered. It soon became apparent that Gauge had an inbuilt desire to learn how to measure anything whatsoever, particularly anything to do with time. He first demonstrated this when he caught sight of the clock on the wall above the door of the kitchen. It was quite an ordinary clock, as clocks go, but the motion of the second hand ticking around seemed to throw the special dragon into a frenzy of delight. He flew out of Liz's hands and hovered in front of it. He tapped the plastic casing. The clock ticked on. Gauge consulted his watch, as if he were using it as a device to check the clock's accuracy. Then something extraordinary happened. Gauge put his watch away and hurred at the clock. Suddenly, its two large hands began to spin, faster and faster, until they were just a blur of black lines.

At the same time, Gauge was copying the movements with his paws. This continued until the clock hands had  spun all the way back to the correct time again. Then it ticked on as if nothing had happened.

Gauge blew a smoke ring and fluttered down onto the kitchen table.

"Mum, what did he just do?" asked Lucy.

Liz ran a finger down the scales on Gauge's spine, a tickling process all the dragons loved. "I think he just learned to tell the time," she said. "Earth time, at least."

"What other time is there?" Lucy asked, wrinkling her nose. She was finding this dragon very puzzling indeed.

Liz just smiled and said, "What time is it, Gauge?"

Gauge stretched his arms and held his paws at the 11:27 position. Perfect, according to the clock.

"Do three o'clock," said Lucy, just to test him.

His paws swept into the correct places.

"Quarter to seven?"

He was spot on again.

"Midnight?"

He clapped his paws together, high above his head.

Lucy made a slight *hmph*. She put her hands behind her back and leaned forward until her nose was almost touching Gauge's snout. "Try…my bedtime," she grinned.

Gauge frowned and looked sideways at Liz.

"That's not fair. He can't know that," said Liz. "Mind you…" She paused a moment and tapped her chin. "Lucy's bedtime is half past eight in the evening, Gauge.

And she's supposed to be asleep no later than nine."

The little dragon sat up and blinked his eyes twice, making a sound like a cash register.

"Why did he do that?" asked Lucy. "Why did he make that noise when he blinked?"

"I can't imagine," Liz said, trying to stop a crafty smile from showing on her face. "Maybe we'll find out later, eh? Now, what are we going to do about the library clock?"

"Who cares about the silly library clock?"

"I do. I think we ought to stage a protest."

Lucy didn't like the sound of that. At school, Miss Baxter had once told the class about a group of women who had chained themselves to railings because they weren't allowed to vote in elections. When Lucy had asked, "What happens when you want to go to the toilet, Miss?" her teacher had said with a flourish, "You just go where you are, my dear!" It was all part of the protest, apparently.

"I'm not being chained to any railings," said Lucy. What if a fly was to land on her nose? Or squirrels hopped up and nipped her ankles? There were lots of squirrels in the gardens next to the library. Besides, if her friends saw her, they would laugh.

"Don't be silly," Liz said. "You can

hand out leaflets while I walk up and down the library precinct with a sign."

"It's Sunday," Lucy pointed out. "No one will be there, Mum. Anyway, it's raining."

Lucy was right about that. The sky had turned a dull grey colour and raindrops were already spattering the windows.

"More time for us to prepare, then," Liz said.

"Time?" Gauge said, pricking his ears.

"Thirteen o'clock," said Lucy.

"Don't tease him," Liz warned her. "You might regret it."

"How?" Lucy snorted. "I'm not frightened of a dragon who times things."

* * *

But Liz was right. Later, Lucy did come to regret her words. As the day crept into evening and the time approached 8:30, she was sitting in the lounge reading a comic when Gauge jumped onto her knee and hurred.

"What?" she asked.

He pointed to the ceiling.

"It's your bedtime," Liz muttered. "Thank you, Gauge."

"I haven't finished my story," Lucy said grumpily. She lifted her comic again.

Gauge spiked her gently with his tail.

"Ow!" she protested.

"Bedtime," her mother repeated.

She hadn't even looked up from the book she was reading. "Go on. I'll be up shortly to tuck you in. And don't forget to brush your teeth."

Lucy put down her comic and stomped upstairs.

When the door had closed Liz said to Gauge, "Teeth cleaning – two whole minutes."

Gauge blinked and made the cashing sound. He flew upstairs.

He kept Lucy at the sink until the toothpaste was practically foaming  from her mouth. He made certain that she brushed, flossed and swilled out – all of which took precisely two minutes.

At nine on the dot, he switched off her light. At eight the next morning, he woke her with a *hrrr* inside her left ear. At breakfast, he timed the perfect boiled egg (three minutes and fifty-eight seconds) and made Lucy chew every mouthful of cornflakes thirty-two times, so that she would not suffer indigestion.

It was driving her mad. "Mum, he's getting on my nerves," she said. "I'm going to chain myself to...the toilet if he doesn't stop timing me!"

"He's just doing his job," Liz said. "There, what do you think about that?" She turned round a large sheet of paper. On it was a rhyme:

TICK TOCK, TICK TOCK,
SAVE THE SCRUBBLEY LIBRARY CLOCK!
IF YOU CARE ABOUT OUR TOWN,
JOIN OUR PROTEST!
JOIN IT NOW!

"Yeah, Mum. Dead impressive."

"I thought so, too," Liz beamed. "I bet lots of people will join in."

Lucy chewed her cornflakes. Thirty, thirty-one, thirty-two. She took another spoonful. "Then what?"

Liz's green eyes sparkled with a hint of mischief. "When we've got enough people on our side, we'll take over the library, sit on the floor and lock ourselves in."

"What?!"

A spit of milk landed on Gauge's snout. He licked it off with one quick sweep of his tongue.

"Mum, have you gone barmy?"

"It's important to protect Scrubbley's traditions, Lucy."

"But we'll be arrested! We'll be in the papers!"

"Mmm, with any luck," Liz said brightly. "We'll probably make the front page. Goodness, I'd better go and brush my hair!"

Chapter Five

Lucy could not believe it. She was going to be a criminal – at the age of nine! She had been to a police station once before when she was four and she had lost her bike. The police officers had been very kind, then, and given her a lollipop because she had cried. But if her mother's plans to storm the town library were successful, the police officers would be sure to take a much dimmer view. She would be put into a prison cell and made to eat porridge. Porridge! Yuk! It was horrible stuff. And they would take her photograph – from her worst side! And make her do inky fingerprints. They might even march her off to court. She would have to see a judge and try not to laugh at his funny wig. It was hopeless. She might be sent to prison for years. All for the sake of a silly clock!

She frowned at Gauge. He was sitting on her bedroom table in front of her, timing her doing her homework. She was supposed to spend half an hour at the weekend on her school cookery project. This week it was a recipe for soup. Lucy had come up with the idea of bacon soup, because she blamed Mr Bacon for telling her mother about the library clock in the first place. The project wasn't going well. She looked at Miss Baxter's notes. *Your soup should make the taste buds tingle whilst still being nutritious. Do not be afraid to experiment with your ingredients!* So far, Lucy's list of ingredients were water and bacon. It didn't sound very tingling at all.

"How long?" she said to Gauge.

"One more Earth minute," he hurred. He glanced at what she'd written. He didn't look impressed.

Lucy wrote the words 'stock cubes' underneath 'bacon'. According to her mother, stock cubes were good with everything. *Rice pudding?* she wondered. *Would they work with milky desserts?*

She sighed. This was ridiculous. Her life was now a series of silly thoughts. But as she glanced at Gauge again and saw the willingness to be helpful in his violet eyes (a quality

that every special dragon possessed)
suddenly an idea came to her.

"Can you mend clocks?" she
asked.

Gauge tilted his head.

"You know, can you take them
apart and put them back together
and make them, y'know, tick
properly again? Or bong?"

Gauge tapped his foot. He wasn't
sure, he said – especially about the
bonging. He wasn't meant to be
a fixing dragon.

"But you could try," said Lucy. "If
I took you to the clock tower you
might be able to make it properly
chime again. Then we wouldn't
have to do the protest, would we?"

Before Gauge could answer, the

doorbell rang and Liz let Henry Bacon into the house. Lucy heard Henry saying that Liz might be interested to know that tomorrow afternoon, in the library, a Mr Trustable of the Scrubbley Town Council was going to present the new plans for the improved clock tower, and would she like to attend? Liz said she would definitely like to attend. Lucy gulped. She felt the end of her pencil snap. She knew exactly what her mother was thinking.

Then Henry said, "Can you help with this, Mrs P? Trying to get a battery into my pocket watch. Very fiddly. Fingers a bit shaky."

"Oh, Lucy's the expert at that kind of thing," Liz said.

Hardly had she called upstairs before Lucy was in the kitchen, panting, "I'll do it!" She shot back up with the watch and the battery before Liz had had time to switch the kettle on.

"There," she said to Gauge, putting it at his feet. "Practise on that."

Gauge looked at it doubtfully. It was a beautiful old watch. It had a cream-coloured face with golden numerals. He didn't want to break it, he said.

Lucy tutted and turned the watch over. Henry had already removed the back plate and flipped the old battery out of its housing. "Just look," she said. "It works off one of these." She broke open the new battery packet. "I expect the library clock's just got…a bigger battery, that's all. Here." She handed it to him.

Gauge took it between his paws. The battery immediately began to crackle and an arc of blue light sparked between his ear tips. A puff of smoke came out of his nostrils. The end of his tail began to jiggle.

"Are you all right?" asked Lucy.

Gauge nodded and put the battery down. Gwendolen, Lucy's own special dragon, who sat in the shadow of her bedside lamp, asked if she might have a go at holding it. Lucy said no and tapped the watch again.

Gauge peered at the workings. He could see two metal wheels with zigzagging teeth all around their perimeters. The wheels were meshed together. Neither wheel was moving, but it was obvious to Gauge that they would do if this energy cell that Lucy called a battery was to power them. He drummed his claws. He felt sure there were more workings underneath the wheels and pointed to another circle of metal that had a straight groove cut across it. There were lots of these, of different sizes, all over the back of the watch.

"They're called screws," said Lucy. "If you turn them, they sort of open."

Gauge's eyes lit up in wonder. This

was a far more interesting timing machine than the clock in the kitchen. He pointed to the screws again, one by one, and to his amazement they began to unwind by themselves.

"Wow, that's clever," gasped Lucy.

Now Gauge grew bolder still. As the screws fell out of their holes, he flipped aside the covering they'd been holding in place to reveal an assembly of wheels and cogs and levers and springs.

Before long, it was all in pieces on Lucy's table.

Suddenly, Liz's voice came drifting up the stairs.

"Lucy, how are you doing with that watch?"

"Nearly done!" Lucy called back. But she was nervous now. "Erm, you can put it back together, can't you?" she asked.

Gauge asked if he could he have a few more Earth minutes to study it.

"No," hissed Lucy. "Stick it all back. Now!"

Gauge frowned in dismay and quickly did as he'd been told.

As soon as the back plate went on Lucy hurried downstairs and handed the watch to Mr Bacon.

"Thank you, child," he said. His eyebrows knotted. "Erm, doesn't appear to be going." He shook it and held it to his ear and looked again. "Dead as a doughnut."

Lucy's cheeks began to flush.

"Must be another duff battery," said Liz.

Mr Bacon sniffed. "You did put the right one in, didn't you, child?"

"Yes!" snapped Lucy, though she remembered the sparks around Gauge's ears and wondered if he might have drained its power.

Just then, Gauge fluttered into the kitchen and landed on the fridge top, looking a bit embarrassed. This time he turned solid as Henry looked around.

Liz didn't even glance at him. But Lucy did. As her mother saw Henry to the door, Lucy gritted her teeth and scowled.

Gauge was holding a watch wheel in his right paw.

Chapter Six

The following afternoon, the grey skies produced a fine drizzle over Scrubbley. It would be enough, Lucy hoped, to put her mother off any daft ideas about marching up and down the library precinct. But Liz was determined. She made Lucy put on her hooded yellow coat. Then she drove them both into town.

The protest sign was by now taped onto a stiff piece of card, which in turn had been tacked, none too securely, to a long wooden stick. Liz sloped it against her shoulder and proudly marched the short distance from the car park to the precinct, chanting her rhyme loudly for all of Scrubbley to hear.

Lucy didn't know where to look. But she did her job, handing out the leaflets her mother had prepared, and was surprised to hear people clapping and saying, "Good on you!" This brought her some cheer. Hopefully it meant they would at least have some visitors when they were hauled off to jail.

If Lucy had expected the precinct to be deserted, she was wrong. A generous crowd had gathered by the library doors. They cheered as Liz trooped down the precinct. One of them dashed forward. To Lucy's dismay, she saw it was her teacher, the barmy Miss Baxter.

"Excellent work!" Miss Baxter gushed, eyeing up Liz's sign. "Hello, Lucy!"

"Hello, Miss," Lucy muttered from deep within her hood.

"Couldn't have come at a better moment," said Miss Baxter. "We've just heard that Councillor Trustable is going to make a short speech out here – for the cameras!"

"Cameras?!" Lucy pushed back her hood. To her horror she saw a film crew. The camera was already pointing at the crowd of protesters.

"They're from the regional TV news," said Miss Baxter.

"Wonderful," said Liz.

"I'm going home," said Lucy.

"No, no," said Miss Baxter, drawing her forward. "It's very

important for people to see that the children of the town are just as willing to preserve the old clock as the adults are."

"But I'm the only 'children' here!" Lucy wailed.

"Then perhaps they'll interview you!" Miss Baxter said.

Interview? Lucy's cheeks turned as pale as the white library walls.

Just then, a round of booing began. Lucy looked up to see a handsome man in a long dark overcoat come strolling purposefully out of the library. He was waving a hand as though people were really cheering, not booing. Beside him was another, shorter man, who looked like some kind of guard.

The handsome man smiled. He had teeth like a run of white piano keys. He stepped onto a small podium. The TV camera swished towards him.

"Ladies and gentlemen—" he began.

"—And children!" cried Miss Baxter, yanking up Lucy's hand.

"And children," he said, with a smarmy sort of nod. "My name is Roger Trustable, your local elected councillor—"

"I didn't vote for you!" someone shouted.

"And this is my companion, Mr Higson." He gestured to the shorter man who rolled his beefy shoulders and sniffed. "We are here today to tell you of a wonderful redevelopment plan for your library."

"Save our clock!" Miss Baxter shouted. The crowd cheered. The camera turned towards them again. (Lucy immediately hid her face.)

Roger Trustable raised an important finger. "The hour beckons and time marches on—"

"Not if you have your way," said Henry Bacon. He was standing, arms folded, by the library doors.

"—Progress must be made."

"Boo!" went Liz.

Lucy gritted her teeth. "Mum," she hissed. The camera was squarely on her mother now. They were going to be on the news!

Liz would not be stopped. "We

don't want progress of the kind you're talking about! We want history! We want our clock restored!"

"Save our clock! Save our clock!" the crowd began to chant.

Councillor Trustable jiggled his tie. "Our reports indicate that the existing clock cannot be repaired—"

"Pah!" Miss Baxter expostulated. "You're just too mean to spend money on it, that's all!"

The Councillor laughed. "If you look at our record over the past two years, madam, you'll see that we've been—"

"Playing the same one!" a heckler shouted.

Lucy did not understand this

remark, but it caused a great ripple of laughter all the same. She looked at Councillor Trustable. His cheeks had flushed. He seemed a little annoyed.

"Perhaps if you were to come into the library and view the Council's plans?" he suggested.

"Oh, we will!" said Liz. And she thrust her stick forward so hard that the cardboard sign came off and struck Councillor Trustable in the chest.

The crowd cheered and surged towards the library doors. Lucy squirmed. The dreaded 'sit-in' had started. Worse still, she could see a police car pulling up on the High Street. All the protesters were now heading for the library, leaving just her, Henry Bacon, the film crew, Councillor Trustable and his guard, Mr Higson, behind. This was it. Her life of crime had begun.

The Councillor stepped down off his podium. His expression was very harsh. He waved the camera away then whispered something snappy to Mr Higson. Higson gave a curt nod and went into the library. He brushed hard past Lucy's shoulder, spinning her round. She turned to find herself in the eye of the camera.

"Want to say something, kid?"

The reporter, a young woman with flyaway hair and very tight blue jeans, thrust a microphone under Lucy's nose.

Lucy gulped. Two policemen strolled past, behind her. In about one minute from now, they would probably come back the other way, carrying her mother kicking and screaming to their waiting car.

"Anything?" the reporter tutted.

Lucy dipped her hand into her deep coat pocket. She brought out Gauge and showed him to the camera. It was time she put her own plans into action. "Dragons rule," she said, and dashed into the library.

Chapter Seven

Lucy couldn't believe her eyes. She had never seen the library so full before – not even on Wildest Read Day when a famous explorer had brought in a snake. The crowd of protesters had swarmed into the gaps between the book shelves.

They were all sitting cross-legged on the floor. All except two: her mother and Miss Baxter. They were standing beside a display board in the Local History section. The two policemen and Henry Bacon were making their way towards them.

"Now then, ladies," one of the policemen began.

"This is a peaceful protest!" said Miss Baxter, wagging a finger as if he were her pupil.

"Not from where I'm standing," the second policeman said. "This is public disorder. If you don't clear the library, we'll have to arrest you."

"Unless they all take out a book," whispered Henry, who was never

74

one to miss an opportunity for a loan.

The policeman waved him aside.

"Boo!" went the crowd. "Save our clock!"

"At least hear us out," Liz said boldly. "We're here to demonstrate how much the people of Scrubbley are against these plans." She pointed to the board, where there were some drawings of Councillor Trustable's proposed new clock.

The first policeman sighed. "Between you and me, madam, I don't care for them either, but invading the library is not the way to get them stopped."

"Then try this," Miss Baxter cried. And she pulled a can of spray paint

from her handbag
and sprayed a
large purple
'X' all over
the plans.

"That's it, you're
nicked," the policeman said.

Miss Baxter promptly sat down
and sprayed his boots purple.

To Lucy's horror, she saw her
mother sit down as well.

That was it. Lucy knew, unless she
acted, all hope was lost. Quickly,
she hurried to the main library desk.
The librarians who normally issued
the books had deserted it to watch the
hilarious goings-on. Lucy slipped
behind it and went to the door which
led to the clock tower above. To her

surprise it was ajar. She peeped inside. It was dark and slightly musty, but she could see a spill of yellow light where the stairs wound upwards. A chill breeze whistled down the old stone steps. Lucy jumped back. She didn't like the dark – or the thought of ghosts. But the thought of going to prison was even worse. She glanced over her shoulder. The policemen were trying to drag Miss Baxter away. Unbelievably, she had stolen their handcuffs and chained herself to a library trolley!

Checking to see that no one was watching, Lucy whispered urgently to Gauge. "Fly up there and see if you can fix the clock. If you only make it properly bong, that will be enough."

Gauge twizzled his nose. He wasn't sure about this. He'd had words with Gruffen before they came out and Gruffen's book had clearly stated that Pennykettle dragons were not to be let loose in human society unless Liz said so. But on this occasion, he didn't have much option.

"Go!" Lucy hissed, and threw him up the stairs.

He fluttered round the curving walls, up towards the light. In a matter of moments he had settled on a dusty wooden platform that was built around the workings of the ancient clock. Its cogs and wheels were huge compared to Mr Bacon's watch. Gauge looked on

in fascination as they ground
slowly round, making a lovely deep
tock every time one of the wheel
teeth engaged.

High above, a pigeon cooed. The
clock groaned and gave a dull sort of

clunk. Gauge knew that it was trying to chime. But something was preventing it. Something unnatural. It was just as if the clock had been wounded in some way. He flew forward to investigate and landed on a rail just beside the main housing. As he did he heard a footstep. Instantly, he turned himself solid.

From the far side of the platform a figure appeared. It was Higson, Councillor Trustable's assistant. Gauge recognised him because he'd watched all the hoo-hah outside through a hole in Lucy's pocket. Higson was carrying a long piece of wood. He kept jabbing it at the clock, trying to wedge it between the wheels. It seemed to Gauge that the

man was trying to break the clock or stop it from working. That made him very angry indeed. He was wondering if he dared risk scorching Higson's ear when a foggy voice said, "Oh no, sir. That won't do the job at all."

Gauge rolled his eyes. From out of nowhere, another figure had appeared. He was very old and had no hair, apart from two bushy growths on either cheek. He was wearing a waistcoat, which had watch chains looping out of both pockets. Gauge smiled. His angry mood lifted. Here was a man who cared about time.

Higson whipped around in surprise. "What the…? Where did you come from?"

"Ah, that is a difficult question," said the figure. "I seem to live here permanently now, if that's any help."

"Who are you?"

"I am Sir Rufus Trenchcombe. Clockmaker to the Crown."

Higson shook his head in confusion. "Are you the, err, keeper of this clock or something?"

Sir Rufus's chest seemed to barrel

with pride. "Indeed, one could say so. Do you have an interest in time-pieces, sir? Were you seeking to release the stuck counter-sprocket by striking it with your planking?"

Higson clicked his tongue. "I was sent here to, err, service it, yeah. This, erm, counter-sprocket. Is that what's wrong with it, then?"

"Indeed so! Faulty these three years past."

Higson lifted his piece of wood. "So if that broke, then…?"

"It would need a vast repair. But the part is sturdy. The King's cannon would surely struggle to break it. 'Tis made from the finest metals in Kent. A greater problem lies with the pendulum arm."

Higson gave an interested nod. "And where's that?"

"Why, there," said Sir Rufus. In a flash, he seemed to disappear and reappear instantly on the other side of Gauge. He pointed to a long piece of rope which dangled down into the depths of the tower. "The balancing weight is missing. If this were adjusted and the counter-sprocket oiled, my clock would run appropriately and the chime would be restored."

"Oh, would it?" Higson grunted.

He sounded disappointed. Then Sir Rufus added, "Of course if the weight be far wrong then the mechanism will altogether stop."

Higson narrowed his eyes.

Suddenly, he noticed Gauge balancing on the rail. Though he was clearly confused and wondering why a clay dragon was in the tower, he nevertheless snatched Gauge up. "How about this for a weight?" He tossed Gauge loosely in his hand.

"A most unlikely prospect," said Sir Rufus.

The man gave a villainous smile. "Let's try it."

Before Sir Rufus could argue, Higson had drawn up the rope, tied Gauge to the end of it and thrown him down the tower shaft, into the darkness. The old clock ground to a weary halt.

Sir Rufus made a strange kind of wailing sound. "Treachery!" he cried. And he stretched out a hand as if to rescue Gauge, but his hand passed straight through the rope.

"Stone me, you're a ghost!" Higson cried. And with a gurgling scream he fled down the stairs, leaving the clock in silence and Gauge still dangling somewhere in the darkness...

Chapter Eight

Until that point, the policemen had been struggling to clear the library. But things were about to change. As Councillor Trustable's assistant burst through the door crying, "A ghost! Help! There's a ghost in the tower!" half the protesters leapt to their feet.

No one needed to be convinced of Higson's sincerity. His hair was as stiff as a row of staples and his face as white as a ping-pong ball. He ran for the glass doors, hit the pane when it didn't open automatically and almost knocked himself out.

"Ghost?" someone queried.

Henry Bacon helpfully put in, "Rumour has it that the spirit of

Sir Rufus Trenchcombe roams the tower. Utter nonsense, of course."

"You're the librarian. Go and look!" someone cried.

Henry glanced uncomfortably at the stairway. "Not in my job description."

Just then, the library clock gave a deep and resounding bong. Then another. And another. And another. And after a few seconds' gap, another.

"The ghost's angry," someone suggested nervously.

But Lucy thought she could hear a joyous wail floating down the stairs. A ghostly breeze whooshed through the library. People screamed and ran for the street. To Lucy's relief, the policeman who'd been escorting her mother to the door buckled at the knees and promptly fainted.

Lucy saw her chance. She tugged her mum's sleeve and whispered, "Mum, I let Gauge go up there."

Liz rolled her eyes. "Then you'd better go and see what he's up to," she hissed.

Lucy ran towards the tower door. "It's all right, I'm not frightened of ghosts," she shouted. And up the steps she pounded – not, of course, expecting to encounter Sir Rufus Trenchcombe at the top.

She stopped by the platform, too scared to even shake. The clock bonged again, almost deafening her.

"Ah, child," said Sir Rufus. "Canst thou free the spirit caught on the rope?" He pointed a wispy finger.

Lucy glanced sideways and saw the pendulum rope jigging about. Suddenly, Gauge appeared. His wings were beating like mad.

He was trying to escape from the shaft but the heavy rope was making it hard for him to fly. With an exhausted *hrrr* he fell back into the darkness. The clock responded with another loud bong.

Lucy ran to his aid. She grabbed the rope and pulled it up to the platform rail. Her nimble fingers quickly released the young dragon. "Are you all right?" she asked.

Gauge shook a cobweb off his tail and nodded. He frowned and turned his head towards the clock. Before Lucy could ask what he was doing, he had flown to the housing and was hurring deeply on one of the big wheels. To her surprise, Lucy saw that a patch of gooey gunge around the wheel was suddenly flowing like oil. The clock gave a heave and the wheel moved freely.

Sir Rufus Trenchcombe whooped with joy. "The counter-sprocket! The dragon creature has released the counter-sprocket. Now the clock may run more keenly."

Lucy stepped forward and stubbed her toe against something on the floor. "Ow, what's this?" She picked up a heavy piece of metal.

"'Tis the weight for the pendulum arm," said Sir Rufus. He pointed to the rope.

"You mean, if I tie this on the end the clock is fixed?" Lucy asked.

"Almost certainly, child."

So Lucy tied on the weight and let

it fall down the shaft. Immediately, the clock gave a sequence of chimes. "It works!" she shouted. "It works! It works!"

Sir Rufus drifted towards the clock's machinery. "Hmm. I fear some adjustment may yet be needed. The warmth of the dragon's breath might have caused some damage to the chime counter."

Gauge gave a *hrrr* that sounded like "Oops". He blew a smoke ring and looked a bit sheepish.

Lucy flapped a hand. "Well, you look after that. I've got to save my mum from going to prison, now."

"A noble gesture," Sir Rufus said, bowing. "I am indebted to you, child." He put out a hand and tried to shake Lucy's. It was a bit scary, watching a ghost hand bobbing up and down through your own, but Lucy was brave and didn't even squeak.

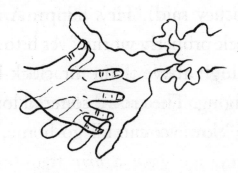

Gathering Gauge to her she said her goodbyes and hurried down the stairs.

To her relief her mum was still there, fanning the policeman who had fainted with a book. "Mum," she cried. "Gauge mended the clock!"

The word quickly went round. Those protesters that were still about shouted hooray.

"What about the ghost, then?" one of them asked.

Lucy said, "He's happy. And the clock properly works." As if to prove it, high above them the clock began to bong. The crowd cheered loudly.

"Now we can all go home," said Lucy.

"Just one second," a smug voice said. It was Councillor Trustable. He turned his wrist and tapped his watch. "I make it four o'clock precisely." He paused and cupped a hand around his ear. "Your clock has just chimed seven…"

Chapter Nine

The next day, it was in all the papers. The protest. Councillor Trustable's new plans. The policeman's purple boots ("Local Teacher Let Off With Warning"). The mystery of the ghost of Sir Rufus Trenchcombe. The strange goings-on with the clock.

Lucy sat, deflated, at the kitchen table, reading one paragraph over again. It said:

Although the Trenchcombe clock appears to be chiming better than it has in years, the sequence is completely wrong. Four o'clock has become seven, eleven o'clock has become three etc, and the clock refuses to bong nine. An expert has said it would be far too costly to change the part required to correct it. The Town Council is therefore recommending that Councillor Trustable's plans be enforced.

Lucy let her head sink onto her arms. "We've failed," she said.

Liz sighed and glanced at Gauge. The young dragon looked terribly crestfallen. "It's no one's fault. We all tried our best. Gauge probably wasn't meant to mend clocks anyway."

Nevertheless, the dragon let his shoulders droop.

"Look, let's go out for a walk," said Liz. "Round the library gardens. We'll take some bread for the ducks."

Lucy sighed. "Only if Gauge can come, too."

Twenty minutes later they were on their way to the library again. Lucy held Gauge to her chest all the way. As they walked down the precinct the little dragon could hardly bear to look at the clock.

But, strangely, as they drew closer, a series of clicks and a few light flashes made him raise his eyes. A large group of people had gathered outside the library again. Most of them were carrying cameras.

"Are they protesters?" Lucy asked her mum.

"No, I think they're tourists," Liz said. "Look, they're all taking photographs of the clock."

The cameras flashed and clicked again.

Lucy pointed to Mr Bacon, who was making an announcement to some of the people. "Next tour of the tower at noon," he was saying. "Five pounds for the chance to see the ghost of Sir Rufus Trenchcombe..."

"Well, I never," Liz said. She chuckled softly. Over to one side of the precinct she could see Councillor Trustable watching the crowd snapping away. He had a thoughtful look on his face. "I think our clock is saved, Lucy. If it becomes a tourist attraction the last thing the Council will want to do is knock it down. It will bring people to the town and make lots of money. It looks like Gauge has succeeded after all." She reached over and tickled his ears.

Hrrr! went the dragon. He flapped a paw.

"Careful," whispered Lucy, "you're supposed to be solid."

"Oh, I think we can forgive him this time," said Liz. And she raised a hand as well and waved at a small arched opening in the tower.

From behind it, Sir Rufus Trenchcombe waved back.

Suddenly, his old clock chimed five times.

Lucy looked at her watch. It was noon, or midday. But from that moment on, lunch time in Scrubbley would always be known as 'five bongs' – all thanks to a dragon named Gauge…

Here's an extract from
the next story about

The Dragons of Wayward Crescent

GLADE

978 1 40830 234 7 £8.99 (hb)
978 1 84616 611 2 £4.99 (pbk)

"Gosh, it's chilly today," Elizabeth Pennykettle said, stamping her feet and blowing on the ends of her fingerless gloves. "Still, these spring weekends are always good for business. How are we doing, Lucy?"

Liz's daughter looked around the covered market stalls. She'd seen more elephants at a water hole than people shopping today. She looked at the rows of clay dragons on her mother's stall then glanced at the open cash tin, which was on an upturned fruit crate beside her. There was a ten pound note and some coins in it. "We've sold two," she said glumly.

"Well, that's two better than none at all," said Liz.

Lucy sighed and pulled on the braids of her bobble hat. She was about to reply when the clock in the tower of the library building gave out three distinct bongs. Anyone who didn't live in the market town of Scrubbley would have thought this rather odd, for it was clearly about eleven o'clock in the morning. But to Lucy, who not only knew the whole sequence of bongs but the reason why the clock always chimed incorrectly, it was no surprise at all. It even helped reinforce what she'd been planning to say, "Mum, we've been standing here for over an hour. I hate doing the market on freezing cold days. My toes are cold. And I think I've got chilblains – on my knees!"

"Well, I'm sorry, but I have to earn a living," Liz said. "We have to eat and pay the bills like anyone else. Making and selling clay dragons is what I do. If you can think of a better job for me, speak up." With that, she leaned across the stall and rearranged a number of her spiky green creations, moving some that had been at the back much closer to the front and placing others in little clusters, on stands.

Another spill of cold air ran though the market place, flapping the bunting on the roofs of the stalls. Lucy shivered and let her hands drift towards a female dragon in the corner of the table nearest her. It was sitting up on its back legs and tail as most of the Pennykettle dragons did. Nearly all of Liz's dragons were characterised in some way. They carried cricket bats or wore a chef's hat, for instance. The dragon nearest Lucy was slightly different. It had a small press of ivy leaves behind one ear. In truth, it was rather an ordinary-looking sculpture. Yet it was the most special of any on the stall. For this pretty little creature was only acting like a piece of solid clay, the way it had been taught to do in human company. But at any given moment it could soften its scales, lift its wings, make fire in the back of its throat and fly. It was real and barely three weeks old. Its name was Glade.

Lucy stretched the cuff of her glove from her wrist and held the gap in front of Glade's snout. Then she made a strange kind of grunting sound, which to most people would have sounded like she had a bad cold. Actually, it was an ancient language called dragontongue, which Lucy and her mother had been able to speak since birth. To Glade's ears the grunt translated as *Hrrr*, which could be interpreted in any number of ways, but which Glade understood to mean, "blow, will you?"

With a quick snuffle, Glade snorted a blast of air, warming Lucy's fingers instantly.

"Hey," said Liz, catching sight of what was happening. "What have I told you about using the special dragons in public?"

Read more stories about

The Dragons of Wayward Crescent

GRUFFEN

978 1 40830 232 3 £8.99 (hb)
978 1 84616 609 9 £4.99 (pbk)

GRABBER

978 1 40830 235 4 £8.99 (hb)
978 1 84616 612 9 £4.99 (pbk)

More books by Chris d'Lacey

The Fire Within
Chris d'Lacey   978 1 84121 533 4   £5.99

Icefire
Chris d'Lacey   978 1 84362 134 8   £5.99

Fire Star
Chris d'Lacey   978 1 84362 522 3   £5.99

The Fire Eternal
Chris d'Lacey   978 1 84616 426 2   £5.99

Dark Fire
Chris d'Lacey   978 1 84616 955 7   £6.99

More Orchard books you might enjoy

Billy Bonkers
Giles Andreae & Nick Sharratt   978 1 84616 151 3   £4.99

Billy Bonkers 2
Giles Andreae & Nick Sharratt   978 1 40830 357 3   £5.99

Beast Quest: Ferno the Fire Dragon
Adam Blade   978 1 84616 483 5   £4.99

Beast Quest: Sepron the Sea Serpent
Adam Blade   978 1 84616 482 8   £4.99

Beast Quest: Arcta the Mountain Giant
Adam Blade   978 1 84616 484 2   £4.99

Beast Quest: Tagus the Horse-Man
Adam Blade   978 1 84616 486 6   £4.99

Beast Quest: Nanook the Snow Monster
Adam Blade   978 1 84616485 9   £4.99

Beast Quest: Epos the Flame Bird
Adam Blade   978 1 84616 487 3   £4.99